God's Love Is Higher Than a Roller Coaster

By Christine Danielewicz

Illustrations by
Beata Banach

Tremendous Leadership
PO Box 267 • Boiling Springs, PA 17007
(717) 701 - 8159 • (800) 233 - 2665 • www.TremendousLeadership.com

Tremendous Leadership's titles may be bulk purchased for business or promotional use or for special sales. Please contact Tremendous Leadership for more information.

Tremendous Leadership and its logo are trademarks of Tremendous Leadership. All rights reserved.

Paperback ISBN: 978-1-961202-25-2
eBook ISBN: 978-1-961202-26-9

DESIGNED & PRINTED IN THE UNITED STATES OF AMERICA

A Note From the Author

When you ride a roller coaster, you might feel excited or afraid. You might laugh or scream or hold your breath. Maybe you cannot wait to get off the ride. Or maybe you wish you could ride the roller coaster over and over again.

You do not get to ride a roller coaster every day, but you do have many different kinds of experiences – things that are fun, things that are boring, things that are easy, and things that are hard. You look forward to some things. You might wish you didn't have to do other things.

You just can't wait for your birthday! You don't always feel like cleaning up your room. You really do not want to be sick or get hurt. When someone who loves you is there with you, the happy times are extra special, the hard things are easier to do, and sadness is shared to bring you strength.

God knows how you feel because he is **omniscient**. That means He knows everything. And somehow He is really there with you because he is **omnipresent**. That means He is everywhere. No matter where you are and no matter what happens, you can say, "God, please help me!" He will hear you, and He will help.

Dedication Page

In memory of my grandparents,
Louis and Anna Finchio "Finocchio"

Grandpa took me to the fair, and Grandma instilled
in me a lifelong love of reading and writing.

Together they taught me about the Gospel
and the love of Jesus Christ.

In memory of Barbara Ann Finchio Crawford
Carpenter, my beautiful mother, friend, prayer
partner, and the woman of God who taught me to
put my faith in the finished work of Jesus Christ on
the cross.

In honor of my beloved sweet William, Bill (Billy) Danielewicz, who waited for me and followed the Lord Jesus in believer's baptism with me, who has been there for me every day and every night for our thus far 35 years of marriage.

In honor of my Aunt Nancy and Aunt Mary Jane, who have nurtured my faith with their prayers and encouragement all of my life.

In memory of my great aunt and great uncles, Veronica (Vera), Joe, John, and Frank Wodka who lived downstairs and always delighted my sister and me with stories, games, long walks, and love as if they had nothing else to do but dote on their nieces.

In memory of a true and faithful friend and sister in the Lord, Caroline Gardner, who devoted her life to teaching the gospel of Jesus Christ to the children of Harrisburg, PA, and Grace Bible Fellowship Church.

Billy woke up on a sunny Sunday morning singing, "This is the day, this is the day that the Lord has made..." Today Grandpa was taking him to the fair after church.

He ran to the window. It was a sunny day! The sky was clear blue. There were no clouds in the sky.

"Hooray!" cried Billy.

1

Billy dashed downstairs into the kitchen.

He told Mom, "Today we are going to the fair! There will be lots of rides. I will go up to the sky on the roller coaster! Then I will ride the merry-go-round. I like the flying swings the best."

"I think you will have fun," said Mom.

Then Dad gave Billy a hug. "You stay close to Grandpa. You will be safe and have fun."

"I love Grandpa Louie," said Billy with a big smile. "I have a dollar in my piggy bank. I will buy Grandpa cotton candy on a stick. He will buy me a foot-long hot dog. We will eat hot dogs and cotton candy and have lots of fun!"

Then Billy remembered something that was not fun.

Tomorrow, Billy had to go to the dentist. He had a cavity – a small hole – in his tooth. Sometimes the tooth hurt.

The dentist would use little tools to fill up
the hole in his tooth. Then the tooth would
not hurt anymore. The dentist would help Billy
with his little tools, but Billy did not know what
the little tools would feel like. Would they be
pointy? Would they be sharp? Billy did not
know, and he felt a little scared.

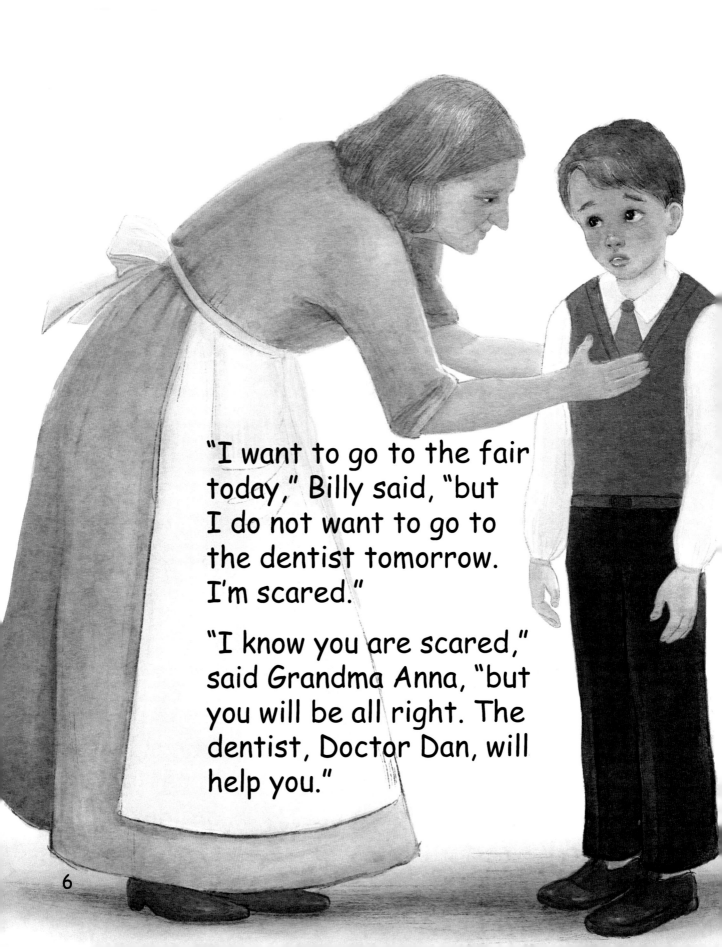

"I want to go to the fair today," Billy said, "but I do not want to go to the dentist tomorrow. I'm scared."

"I know you are scared," said Grandma Anna, "but you will be all right. The dentist, Doctor Dan, will help you."

6

"We will pray for you," Grandma Anna told Billy. "Jesus will be with you at the fair to help you have fun, and He will be with you at the dentist to help you be brave."

"OK," sighed Billy.

"Hurry now," Grandma smiled as she tickled his tummy. "Finish getting ready for church. We need to be there soon."

Billy got ready for church quickly. He wore his best white shirt, red vest, black pants and a shiny black belt.

After he combed his hair and tied his shoes, he washed his face and brushed his teeth. He was ready to go!

Mom, Dad, and Billy sang songs as Dad drove them to church. They sang, "Jesus loves me, this I know, for the Bible tells me so."

They sang, "God is so good. God is so good. God is so good; he's so good to me. God loves me so. God loves me so. God loves me so; he's so good to me." Billy liked to sing about God. He loved Jesus.

9

At church, Billy saw many of his friends:
Eddie, Mark, Pete, Heidi, Lorraine,
Debbie, Mike, Chrissy, Chuck, Cindy,
Stevie, and another Heidi.

His Sunday school teachers, Miss Patty and Mrs. Caroline, began to read a true Bible story about Jesus from the Bible. Billy could not wait to hear the story.

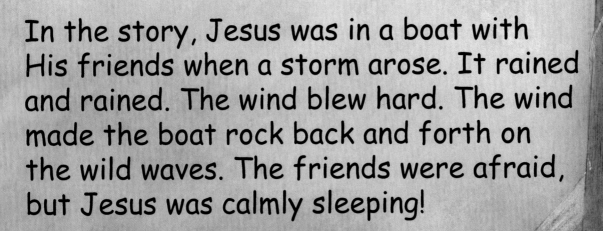

In the story, Jesus was in a boat with His friends when a storm arose. It rained and rained. The wind blew hard. The wind made the boat rock back and forth on the wild waves. The friends were afraid, but Jesus was calmly sleeping!

The friends woke Jesus up.

Jesus said, "Don't be afraid," and He told the storm to stop. The rain stopped falling. The wind stopped blowing. The boat stopped rocking. His friends were happy that the storm had ended. They felt safe with Jesus.

He thought about the rides. He thought about the roller coaster high up in the sky. He thought about the hot dogs and cotton candy.

He could hardly wait! When Pastor Jeff was done teaching, all the people sang, "This is the day that the Lord has made! Let us rejoice and be glad in it!" Billy really was glad!

Then Billy was off to the fair with Grandpa. He sat next to Grandpa in his big, blue pickup truck. Grandpa told funny stories on the way to the fair. Billy and Grandpa laughed and chatted all the way to the fair.

Billy and Grandpa saw Eddie, Mark, Mike, and Pete when they got to the fair. Billy and his friends rode the roller coaster first.

"Let's ride high up to the sky!" Billy shouted. Grandpa Louie was waiting for them at the exit gate when they got off the roller coaster. Then Billy's friends dashed over to the Ferris wheel.

"See you later," they called as they hurried over to the next ride.

Billy and Grandpa went to the merry-go-round next.

Billy's neighbor, Chrissy, shouted, "Hey, Billy, wait for me!" Billy rode a white horse with a black mane and tail while Chrissy chose a tan horse. Grandpa stood next to Billy's horse. Around and around they went.

"Hurry, Grandpa," Billy urged as he hopped off his horse at the end of the ride. "Let's go on the flying swings next. That's the ride I like best!"

"All right," Grandpa Louie agreed. "Let's go!"

When they got to the swings, Grandpa said, "You get in line, and I'll watch you."

Billy waited in line. Soon it was his turn. He jumped up into a shiny green swing. He waved to Grandpa the first time he went around.

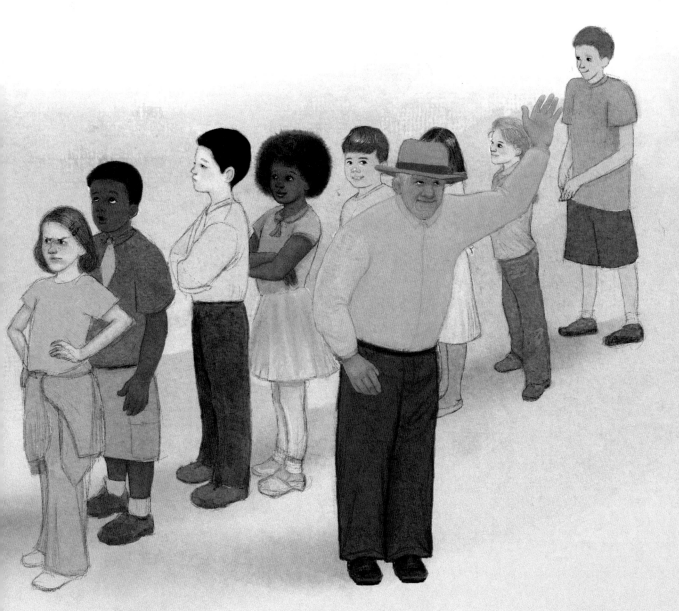

He waved again the second time. Billy was having so much fun that he forgot to wave after that.

Soon the swings slowed down and then came to a stop. Billy got off his swing and ran to the exit gate.

He looked for Grandpa, but Grandpa was not there! Billy looked around, but he could not see Grandpa. Billy was scared! He did not know what to do. He did not know where to go. So, he stood still and waited for Grandpa.

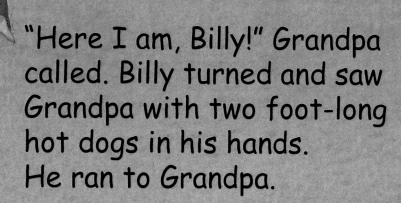

"Here I am, Billy!" Grandpa called. Billy turned and saw Grandpa with two foot-long hot dogs in his hands.
He ran to Grandpa.

"Why do you look so scared?" asked Grandpa. He smiled warmly, "I told you I would watch you. The hot dog stand is right next to the swings. You could not see me, but I could see you. I love you, Billy. I would never leave you all alone."

29

Billy hugged Grandpa. "I love you, too, Grandpa Louie! Thank you for the hot dogs."

30

After they ate the hot dogs, Billy said, "I have a dollar, Grandpa. I will buy you some cotton candy."

"Thank you, buddy," Grandpa said with a smile. "I will share it with you. What color should we get?"

"Blue, please!" shouted Billy.

Billy and Grandpa ate tasty hot dogs and sticky cotton candy. They rode rides all day long.

When it got dark, they watched fireworks light up the sky with bright colors—red, blue, green, purple, and gold.

Then Grandpa took Billy home. Billy was so tired that he fell asleep in the truck. Grandpa carried him into his house, and Dad carried him up to bed.

"Good night, Grandpa," Billy whispered as Grandpa handed him to Dad.

"Good night, buddy," Grandpa said as he kissed him good night.

When Billy woke up, he got dressed, and Mom drove him to the dentist.

"Hop up in the big chair, Billy," said Doctor Dan. "I'll fix that tooth, so it will not hurt anymore."

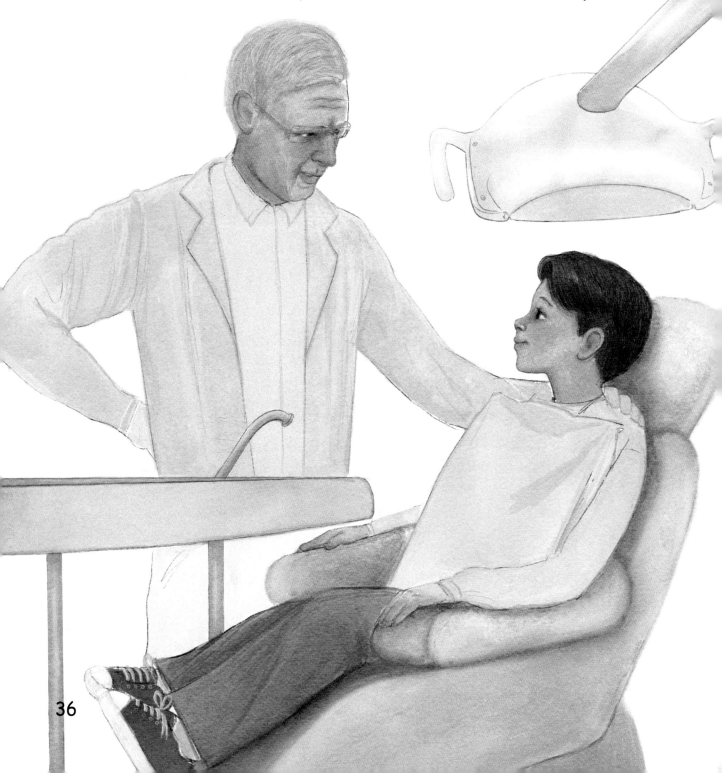

Billy sat in the big chair. He looked at Doctor Dan's light and his tools. He began to feel scared. Grandma Anna had said that Jesus would be with him to help him be brave, but Billy did not see Jesus.

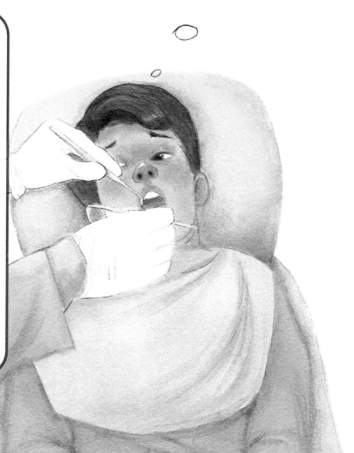

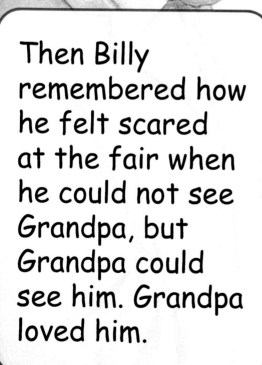

Then Billy remembered how he felt scared at the fair when he could not see Grandpa, but Grandpa could see him. Grandpa loved him.

Billy felt better. He knew Jesus could see him, and Jesus would help him. He remembered Grandma Anna's prayer and the true Bible story from Miss Patty's and Mrs. Caroline's Sunday school class. Jesus's friends felt safe with Him in the boat. Billy felt safe with Grandpa, and now he felt safe with Jesus, too. Jesus loved him.

Doctor Dan fixed Billy's tooth. The little tools felt strange in his mouth. Doctor Dan's light was bright. The tools made a lot of noise, but Billy was all right. He was safe with Jesus.

While Doctor Dan worked on his tooth, Billy thought about the fair. The roller coaster is the highest ride. Billy thought about Jesus. Jesus loved him all the way from heaven. Jesus's love is even higher than a roller coaster!

40

"LORD, Your faithful love reaches to heaven,
Your faithfulness to the clouds."
Psalm 36:5 (HCSB)

About the Author

Christine Danielewicz is a secretary who enjoys supporting all areas of ministry at Grace Bible Fellowship Church in Harrisburg, PA, where she and her husband, Bill, are members.

While growing up in Northwest Pennsylvania, her grandfather, Louie, took her, along with her sister and cousins, to the Perry Hi-Way Hose Company's summer fair every year. Her favorite ride was called the Flying Swings. She remembers when her ride had ended and she jumped down from her swing to rejoin Grandpa…but could not find him! For a moment, she was so scared! Then she realized that Grandpa Louie was right there all along, even though she could not see him. When she grew up, this became an object lesson to remind her of God's love and constant presence.

Chris began writing in second grade, curled up on the sofa at home with a drawing tablet or scrunched into a cozy chair in the school library with a notebook, scrawling pages and pages of poems and adventure stories. In 1982, she became a teacher and taught in public and private schools for many years. She has also been involved in home education, children's church clubs and camps, and her private piano studio, where she taught students aged 2 to 90.

Above all, Chris has most enjoyed family time with her husband and their three children through all the stages and seasons of life. God has been faithful in the beautiful joys, the uncertain times, and the crushing disappointments.

The Scripture that anchors her life is Galatians 2:20-21, "I have been crucified with Christ. It is no longer I who live, but Christ who lives in me. And the life I now live in the flesh I live by faith in the Son of God, who loved me and gave himself for me. I do not nullify the grace of God, for if righteousness were through the law, then Christ died for no purpose" (NASB).

About the Illustrator

Beata Banach is a professional artist and illustrator born in Lublin, Poland. Art has been her favorite thing to do since childhood. She's always been inspired by the outdoors and nature. Beata has six years of experience in illustrating children's books. She specializes in traditional mediums such as watercolors, oils, gouache, and pencils.

Beata also works digitally and likes to mix those two mediums. She received her master's in Fine Arts in 2018 from the Marie Curie-Sklodowska University in Poland, where she majored in traditional easel painting.

Made in the USA
Middletown, DE
25 October 2024

63134118R00029